Pip and the Ge...

Created by Keith Chapman

First published in Great Britain by HarperCollins Children's Books in 2008

1 3 5 7 9 10 8 6 4 2
ISBN-13: 978-0-00-726534-3
ISBN-10: 0-00-726534-4

A CIP catalogue record for this title is available from the British Library.

Based on the television series *Fifi and the Flowertots*
and the original script 'Pip and the Genie' by Wayne Jackman
© Chapman Entertainment Limited 2008

Printed and bound in China
Visit Fifi at: www.fifiandtheflowertots.com

Pip and the Genie

HarperCollins *Children's Books*

Fifi was busy weeding her garden. "I can't plant my beans until I've dug up all the weeds," she said to herself, "but I could really do with some help!"

"Looks like you've got your work cut out there, Fifi!" laughed Stingo. "I know," she sighed. "I've got too many jobs to do today. I was hoping to make a blackberry pie, too. But I don't think I'll have time."

"You get started on the weeding then, Slugsy," said Stingo. "And I'll go and think of a plan to get out of the rest of the jobs." And away he flew.

Webby was reading Pip a story. "...and so the genie told Aladdin that if he ever wanted a wish to come true, he just had to rub the magic lamp and the genie would appear. The End."

"Wow!" said Pip, "I"d do anything to meet a genie!" "Would you now Pip?" murmered Stingo, from his hiding place. "Hmmm..."

"Look what I found, Bosss," said
Slugsy when Stingo returned.
"Just what I need, Slugsy - a magic lamp! Now all
I need is a genie. Let's get you dressed up!"

Slugsy didn't feel much like a genie, but he did as he was told. He hid in the grass while Stingo went to find Pip. "Hey, Pip," called Stingo, "come and see what Slugsy just dug up!"

"What is it?"
asked Pip.
"A magic lamp!"
said Stingo. "I'll give
it to you if you do
some jobs for us!"
"Wow!" said Pip, "but how
do I know it's magic?"
"Rub it and see,"
grinned Stingo.
Pip did. First there was
a cloud of flour, and then
the genie appeared!
"Whoo," it said, "I am the
genie of the lamp.
Your wish is my...er..."
"Command?" said Pip.
"you're not a very
good genie."

"He's been stuck inside the
lamp for a long time, Pip,"
said Stingo quickly. "He'll get better."
"Oh, I see, " said Pip, "so what
jobs do I have to do?"

"Then why is Pip outside doing them?" asked Bumble. "Why are you weeding the garden, Pip?" asked Fifi. "Because Stingo said he'd give me his magic lamp if I did the jobs on the list. It's got a genie in it!" "But there's no such thing as a genie, Pip," Fifi said, gently.

"Never mind, Pip, " said Bumble. "If I can help you with the jobs we'll get them done twice as fast. Then Fifi can carry on baking."

"Thanks both of you", said Fifi. "We can all have blackberry pie! But I think we'll give Stingo a taste of his own medicine..."

Bumble and Pip soon
finished all the chores, and
Fifi came out with a beautiful
blackberry pie.

"Thank you both so much for doing all my jobs", she said. "Have a slice of pie! And while you're eating it, I'll tell you how we're going to teach Stingo a lesson!"

Stingo was looking
through his telescope
when suddenly he noticed
the three friends eating
Fifi's blackberry pie.

"Hey Slugsy, Pip's finished all the jobs already –
and he's eating our pie! Let's get over
there quickly!" Stingo yelled.
"Yes bosss", said Slugsy, obediently.

"He said I could wish for anything I wanted, so I wished for him to help me with all the jobs. He got them done in no time!"

"How about swapping that silly old honey pot for this delidious pie, Pip?" asked Stingo.
"OK," said Pip.

Stingo grabbed the honey pot and began to rub it.
"Come on genie! Watch this, Slugsy!"

Suddenly the genie appeared -
it was Bumble dressed up.
But Stingo didn't know that.
"Bingo Stingo!" he said, "I've got my own genie!"
"I'm the genie of the honey pot," said the genie.
"Your wish is *NOT* my command!"
"But you have to do everything I want!" said Stingo.

"Do I?" asked Bumble, dropping his disguise.
"Bumble!" exclaimed Stingo. "Bumble is the honey genie?"
"It was Bumble who helped Pip do all the jobs, Stingo,"
said Fifi. "There's no such thing as a real genie.
But real friends don't play tricks on each other.
They help each other out. You should try it some time –
you'll be amazed at what can get done!"

Grow your own bean plant

You can grow your own bean plant, just like Fifi!

You will need:

* A bean
* Small stones
* A plant pot
* Soil
* Water
* A tray or saucer

1. Find some stones slightly larger than the holes in the plant pot, and put them in the bottom.

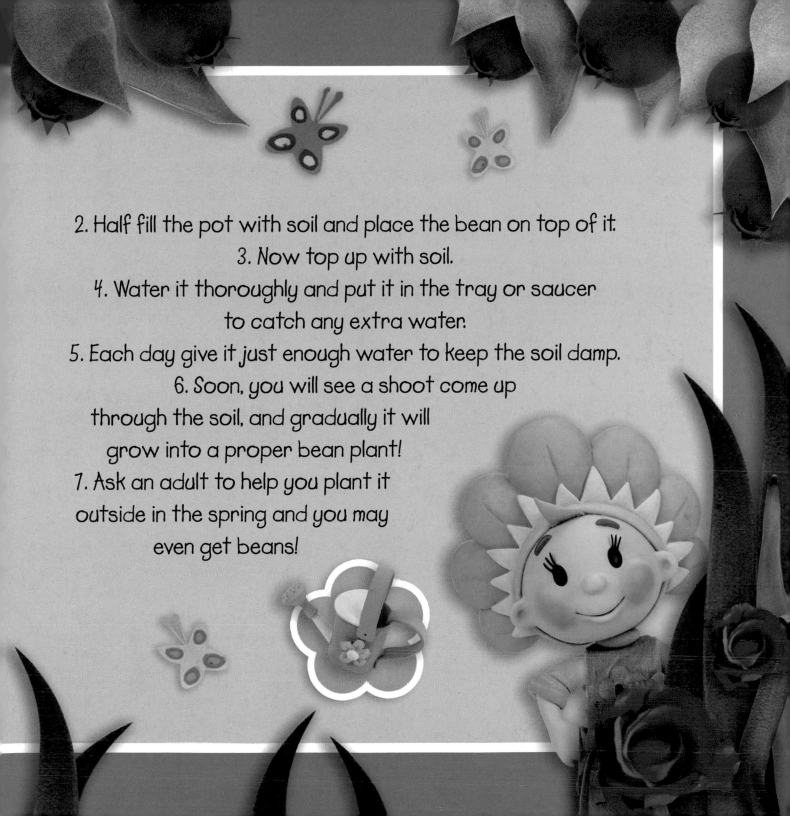

2. Half fill the pot with soil and place the bean on top of it.

3. Now top up with soil.

4. Water it thoroughly and put it in the tray or saucer
to catch any extra water.

5. Each day give it just enough water to keep the soil damp.

6. Soon, you will see a shoot come up
through the soil, and gradually it will
grow into a proper bean plant!

7. Ask an adult to help you plant it
outside in the spring and you may
even get beans!